DOORWAY TO WONDERFUL FUN
AS LONG AS YOU ARE ALLOWED
TV ACCESS.

I HATE TV-TURNOFF WEEK.
LAMEST IDEA YET.

Zeke Meeks is published by
Picture Window Books
A Capstone Imprint
1710 Roe Crest Drive
North Mankato, Minnesota 56003
www.capstonepub.com

Library of Congress Cataloging in Publication Data
Green, D. L. (Debra L.)
  Zeke Meeks vs. the horrifying TV-Turnoff Week / by D. L. Green;
illustrated by Josh Alves.
       p. cm. — (Zeke Meeks)
  Summary: It is Television-Turnoff Week, and Zeke and his friends are
wondering what they will do with their time without their favorite programs
and videogames.
  ISBN 978-1-4048-6804-5 (library binding)
  ISBN 978-1-4048-7220-2 (pbk.)
 1. Television and children—Juvenile fiction. 2. Recreation—Juvenile fiction.
3. Schools—Juvenile fiction. [1. Television—Fiction. 2. Recreation—Fiction.
3. Schools—Fiction. 4. Humorous stories.] I. Alves, Josh, ill. II. Title. III. Title:
Zeke Meeks versus the horrifying TV-Turnoff Week. IV. Title: Zeke Meeks vs.
the horrifying Television-Turnoff Week.

  PZ7.G81926Zf 2012

  813.6—dc23   2011029903

Vector Credits: Shutterstock
Book design by K. Fraser

Printed in the United States of America in Stevens Point, Wisconsin.
102011   006404WZS12

I'M COMING
FOR YOU
ZEKE . . .

WHO IN THEIR RIGHT MIND
WOULD HAVE A PET BUG?

IF YOU THINK YOU'LL FIND
ME WEARING THIS HAT IN
THIS BOOK, DREAM ON.

TABLE OF

EVERYTHING BUT THE PLAYGROUND

BOYS RULE

ME, LOOKING EXTREMELY BORED

CONTENTS

GIRLS DROOL ALL BUT GRACE – SHE BITES

A TRILLION TIMES Worse

Than an Ice Cream Party

The day started out great. For one thing,
I had gotten my best grade ever on a math test:
a C+. *Yahoo!*

For another thing, it was Friday. I was going
to my best friend Hector's house after school.
Then I planned to sit around and watch TV and
play video games all weekend. I couldn't wait.

For a third thing . . . wait. I'm confused.
Maybe that's the fourth thing. I'm not very good
at math.

Anyway, for another thing, recess was really fun. Hector and I pretended we were Enemy Warriors from the *Fight, Fight, Fight* TV show.

On the show, Enemy Warriors zoomed around Planet Fatal and stabbed each other with red-hot electro-swords. Hector and I ran around the school playground and stabbed each other with invisible swords.

I was running so fast that I almost crashed into Grace Chang. It wasn't really my fault. Grace is so tiny that I didn't notice her at first.

But she noticed me. She yelled, "Zeke Meeks! Get out of my face."

"Yeah. Get out of her face," Emma G. said.

"Yeah. Get out of her face," Emma J. said.

"Get out of my face" was a line from the *Sassy Sara* TV show. A lot of kids in my third-grade class watched that show. Sassy Sara often shouted, "Get out of my face," or "Get your face out of my space" or "Get lost and don't ever be found."

I pretended to slash Grace with my invisible sword. She dug the nail on her pinky finger into my arm.

That may not seem too bad. But Grace Chang has extremely long and extremely sharp fingernails. So when her pinky nail dug into my arm, it was extremely painful.

And that's when my great day started to get terrible.

After recess ended, our teacher, Mr. McNutty, said, "I have four announcements. And they are all good."

Hector raised his hand and asked, "Are we going to have an ice cream party?"

"You're close," Mr. McNutty said.

"Are we going to a candy factory?" I guessed.

"You're close," Mr. McNutty said.

"Are we getting more time for recess?" Laurie Schneider asked.

"Close," Mr. McNutty said. "I'll just tell you the news. We're having a week of no—"

Owen Leach interrupted him.

A WEEK OF NO HOMEWORK!

"A week of no tests!" Aaron Glass shouted.

"You're both close," Mr. McNutty said. "We're having a week of no TV or video games. We'll begin TV-Turnoff Week tomorrow. I've already e-mailed your parents about it."

Everyone groaned. A week of no TV or video games was not at all close to a week of no homework or tests. It was as far away as another universe, a very bad universe. Also, announcing TV-Turnoff Week was not good news. It was very bad news.

"Watching *Fight, Fight, Fight* is the only good part of my day," Chandler Fitzgerald said. Then he started to cry.

AWKWARD!

Chandler cried a lot. He cried yesterday because it rained. He cried the day before because his pencil needed to be sharpened. But today, he cried louder than usual.

"You, get lost . . . NOW!" Grace Chang said. "That's from *Sassy Sara*, my favorite show. I won't know what to do without it."

"Yeah. Me neither," Emma G. said.

"Yeah. Me neither," Emma J. said.

Mr. McNutty said, "You can find better things to do with your time. TV-Turnoff Week is the first good news. The second good news is that you'll each give an oral report. You'll tell the class about what you did instead of watching TV."

"I already know what I'll be doing: crying," Chandler cried.

"I'll be so angry I'll tear people's faces off," Grace Chang said.

I didn't cry very often. And I had never torn off a single face. But during a week without TV or video games, I probably would cry. I might even tear off a face or two. I might even cry and tear someone's face off at the same time. That's how upset I'd probably get.

"The third good news is that we will have a spelling bee on Thursday. The fourth good news is that the winner will get a gift certificate to a bookstore. So make sure you study," Mr. McNutty said.

SPELLING BEE

DOES MR. MCNUTTY EVEN KNOW WHAT GOOD NEWS IS?

None of these things were good news. I didn't even want a gift certificate to a bookstore. I didn't like bookstores. That's because bookstores had books in them. And I didn't like books. I liked TV. In fact, I loved TV.

I told Hector I couldn't come to his house after school. I wanted to stay home and watch TV nonstop, before TV-Turnoff Week started.

So I watched TV all afternoon and evening. I saw some of my favorite shows: *The Talking Underwear*, *Wolfboy*, and *Super Force Field*. During the commercials, I played video games.

I even watched my little sister Mia's favorite show, *Princess Sing-Along*. That show is about a bratty princess who sings lame songs in a screechy voice. It should be called *Princess Screech-Along*.

The princess screeched the same two songs over and over. The first one was: "If you must pass gas, la la la, don't do it in class, la la la." The second song was: "Don't walk outside in your bare feet, la la la. There could be dog doo in the street, la la la." I couldn't get the songs out of my head. But watching *Princess Sing-Along* was still better than not watching TV at all.

I had a hard time falling asleep that night. I had too much on my mind. I didn't know how I could ever last an entire week without TV.

The other things on my mind were: "If you must pass gas, la la la, don't do it in class, la la la." And, "Don't walk outside in your bare feet, la la la. There could be dog doo in the street, la la la."

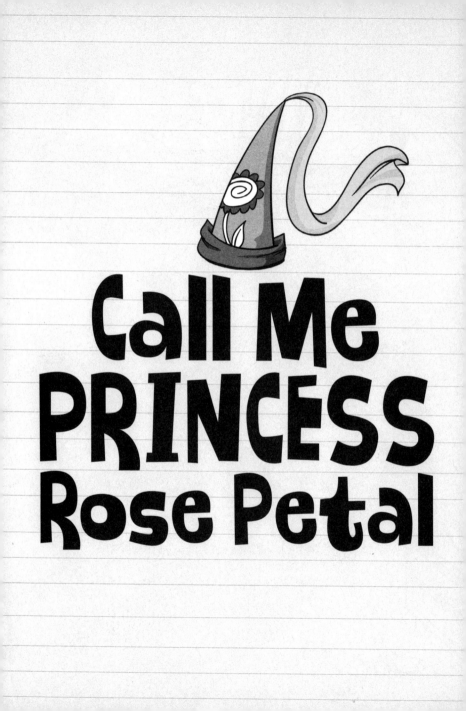

Call Me PRINCESS Rose Petal

When I awoke on Saturday morning, I sang, "Don't walk outside in your bare feet, la la la. There could be dog doo in the street, la la la." I told you I couldn't get the lame Princess Sing-Along songs out of my mind.

Then I remembered that TV Turnoff Week had begun. I didn't know what to do without TV or video games. I wondered what time it was. I moved a book that was blocking the clock on my dresser. It was only 6:15 in the morning.

I stared at the ceiling for awhile. I couldn't think of anything else to do.

Finally, I got out of bed and went to the living room. My little sister, Mia, was sitting on the rug. She was looking through some picture books.

I plopped on the sofa and rested my feet on a stack of books on the coffee table. "I don't know what to do," I told Mia.

She looked up from her picture book. "What? I didn't hear you. I was very busy looking at my book."

"There's nothing to do without TV or video games. I'm bored," I said. I moved a book out of the way. Then I lay down on the couch.

"You could read a book," Mia said.

THIS IS WHAT BORED LOOKS LIKE.

"No. I'm bored, but I'm not desperate," I replied.

"Speaking of bored, let's play a board game," she said.

"No thanks." I shook my head. Mia was too young for the board games I liked.

"Do you want to play with my Princess Sing-Along doll?" she asked.

I shook my head harder.

"We could have a tea party," Mia said.

I shook my head even harder.

"We could dress up like princesses," Mia said.

I shook my head even harder.

"Or we could sing some Princess Sing-Along songs," said Mia.

I shook my head so hard it almost fell off my neck. Then I said, "Okay. I'll play a board game with you."

"Yay!" Mia squealed. She brought over her Princess Sing-Along board game. Then she sat next to me on the couch.

THIS IS WHAT SUPER BORED LOOKS LIKE.

I wished there was something else to do. But I crawled onto the floor and got the game ready.

Mia pointed to the cardboard game pieces. "I'll be Princess Sweet Cheeks. Do you want to be Princess Rose Petal, Princess So Beautiful, or Princess Pink Blossom?"

I sighed. "I guess I'll be Princess Rose Petal," I said.

"She's pretty," Mia said.

We spun a wheel with numbers on it. The number told us how many spaces to move the princesses forward or back. The first princess who went from the dungeon to the castle would win.

It is really hard to get excited about a game where no matter if you win or lose, you are still a princess. I mean, who cares? Still, what else did I have to do?

It took Mia a really long time to spin the wheel and count her spaces. After an hour, neither Princess Sweet Cheeks nor Princess Rose Petal was anywhere near the castle. "How long does it usually take to finish the game?" I asked.

"Not long," Mia said. "Usually just a week or two."

I groaned. "I'm done," I said. "If I try to play anymore, my eyes are going to fall out from boredom. You win."

"Yay!" said Mia.

Our dog, Waggles, came into the room. He carried a book in his mouth. He was wearing a pink and purple striped sweater.

Mia said, "I dressed up Waggles this morning. Doesn't he look great?"

"No," I said.

"Waggles brought you a book," Mia said.

I shook my head. "Books are dumb. But playing with Waggles is fun."

I spent the next hour tossing balls to Waggles. It was fun for the first five minutes. It was okay for the next fifteen minutes. It was really, really boring for the last forty minutes.

I had gone only a few hours without TV and video games. And I was already really, really bored. I didn't know how I could ever survive the entire TV-Turnoff Week.

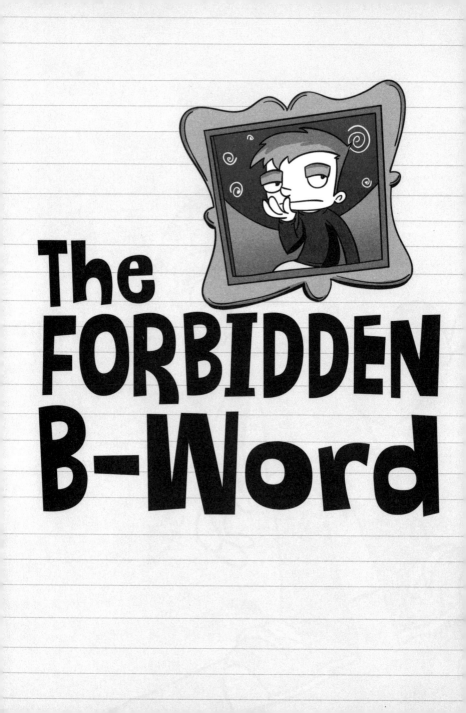

The FORBIDDEN B-Word

It was still Saturday morning, the first day of TV-Turnoff Week. My sisters, Alexa and Mia, were in the living room with Mom and me.

"I'm so bored," I said for about the twentieth time.

"I'm bored of hearing how bored you are," Mom said.

"Well, I'm bored of hearing you're bored of hearing how bored I am," I said.

My older sister, Alexa said, "I'm bored of hearing you tell Mom that you're bored of hearing Mom say she's bored of hearing how bored you are."

"Huh?" my little sister, Mia, asked.

"I'm bored," I said again.

Mom groaned. Then she said, "I'll take you somewhere fun today. But only if you promise not to say you're bored for the rest of the day."

"Okay. Can we go to Tunnels, Slides, and Balls Galore?" I asked.

In case you don't know, Tunnels, Slides, and Balls Galore has tunnels, slides, and balls galore in it.

"Tunnels, Slides, and Balls Galore is boring," Alexa said. "Let's go shopping instead."

"Shopping is boring," Mia and I said.

WE'RE GOING TO THE ART MUSEUM!

"Art museums are boring," Alexa, Mia, and I all said. That was only the second time ever that my sisters and I had all agreed on something. The first time was when we all agreed that liver tasted disgusting.

Mom made us go to the art museum anyway.

To my surprise, it wasn't boring. It was much better than sitting at home and complaining about being bored.

My favorite paintings had cool fighting soldiers on them. My dad is a soldier. He was away on a top-secret mission. He's even cooler than the soldiers in the art museum paintings.

My sister Alexa liked the modern art paintings. They were very simple pictures that didn't make much sense. One looked like someone had spilled paint all over it. Another one was just a big red square with a messy orange border.

Mia pointed to them and said, "These look like paintings I did in preschool last year. But I'm a much better artist now." Then she laughed and pointed to a picture of a naked lady. "That's funny," she said.

"That's gross," I said.

My mom showed me a painting of flowers. I thought it was boring. But I didn't say that. I'd promised not to say "boring" today.

"Look closely at the painting. It's made up of thousands of tiny dots," Mom said.

I peered at it and saw the tiny dots. The painting wasn't boring after all. It was really cool. But it would have been even cooler if the tiny dots formed fighting soldiers instead of flowers.

Once we got home from the museum, I told my mom, "Thanks for taking us to the art museum. But now I'm bo . . . I'm the b-word again."

"Clean out your closet. That will keep you busy," she said.

"That sounds bo . . ." I stopped myself from saying boring. Then I said, "That sounds tedious, dull, tiresome, and dreary. It also sounds like a word that rhymes with snoring."

"You might find some interesting things in your closet," Mom said.

I shook my head. "No I won't."

But I did. I found Halloween candy that I had hidden three years ago and had forgotten about. The candy was so hard it nearly cracked my teeth. But it still tasted good.

OUCH!

I also found a yo-yo and some books in my closet. I played with the yo-yo. Then I did a puzzle from my crossword puzzle book and a word search from my word search book.

"Zeke!" Mom shouted from the doorway of my bedroom.

"You don't have to shout," I said.

"I have to shout when you ignore me. I've been calling you for dinner," said Mom.

"First can you help me with my crossword puzzle? What's a word for something that can dull people's brains? It only has two letters in it," I said.

"TV," she said.

I shook my head. "TV can't dull people's brains."

"See if the word *TV* fits in your crossword puzzle," Mom said.

I did. The word fit.

"Thanks. Now what's a seven-letter word for something that makes people smarter?" I asked.

"Reading," Mom said.

I shook my head again. "That can't be right. Reading doesn't make people smarter."

"Try the word *reading* in your crossword puzzle," she said.

I did. It fit.

"Now come to dinner," Mom said.

"Okay. At least eating dinner will give me something to do," I said.

"It seems that you've been very busy today," she replied.

I crossed my arms and said, "I'd rather be watching TV. I can't wait for this week to be over."

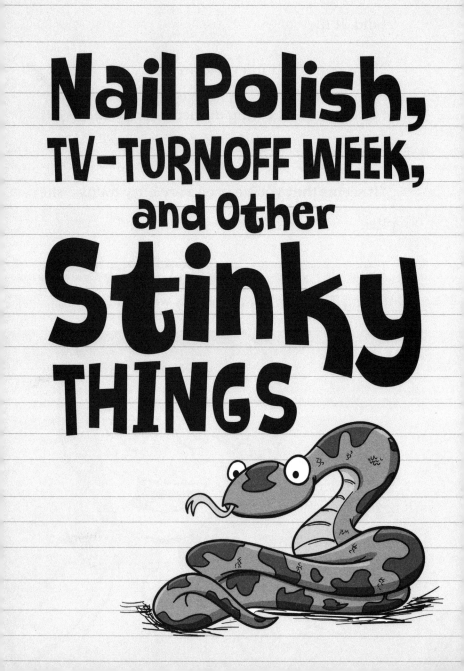

I woke up on Sunday morning and rushed out of bed to see *Fight, Fight, Fight* on TV.

Then I remembered it was TV-Turnoff Week. I let out a big sigh.

Then I played with my yo-yo.

After that, I worked on another crossword puzzle. I couldn't figure out one of the words. The clue was "Type of snake." The word started with a P and had six letters in it.

You don't know what the word is, do you? If you do, you're a lot smarter than me.

I'll give you time to think about it.

Are you thinking?

Are you?

Did you figure it out yet?

I thought about it a lot. But I still didn't know what type of snake started with a P and had six letters in it.

Then I remembered a book I'd found in my closet yesterday. The book was called *Snakes*. I had never read it, of course. I got it for my birthday last year from someone who didn't know me very well. Anyone who knew me well knew that I didn't like books.

But I got out the book, looked through it, and found the answer to the crossword puzzle.

Are you ready for the answer?

I'm giving you two more seconds.

Now are you ready?

Okay, it's . . .

WHO KNEW I COULD SMILE AND READ AT THE SAME TIME?

ARE YOU SURE YOU'RE READY?

The type of snake with six letters that starts with a P is python.

My *Snakes* book had a cool picture of a python in it. It also had cool pictures of vipers, cobras, and other kinds of snakes.

I kept looking at the snake pictures and reading the words next to them. I ended up reading the whole book. I couldn't help it.

Hmm. Maybe the person who'd given me the snake book really did know me very well.

After I finished the snake book and the crossword puzzle, I went into the living room. The room smelled awful. It smelled almost as awful as the Meat Dish Surprise that Mom had made for dinner last week.

My older sister, Alexa, was sitting on the couch. On her lap was our dog, Waggles. He wore a purple bow on his head. He looked very silly.

WHAT'S MAKING THAT YUCKY STINK?

"You mean that lovely aroma?" Alexa asked.

"No. I mean that yucky stink," I said.

"You might be sniffing the sweet scent of my lavender nail polish," she said.

"Did you polish your nails in here?" I asked.

"Yes," she said. "And I was so bored that I painted Waggles's nails, too."

I looked at Waggles's nails. They were purple. They matched the silly bow on his head. "Poor Waggles," I said.

ACK!!! ATTACK OF THE STINKY POLISH!

"Can I polish your nails, too, Zeke?" Alexa asked.

"No," I said. I picked up a book from the coffee table to use as a shield.

"How about your toenails?" Alexa asked.

"No." I picked up another book to make a thicker shield.

"Can I just polish one little toenail of yours?" Alexa asked.

"No," I said.

"But I'm bored," she said.

"I'm bored, too. But I'll never, ever, ever be bored enough to get my nails polished," I said.

Our little sister, Mia, came into the room. She was loudly screeching a Princess Sing-Along song. "If you get up early in the day, la la la, waking your parents is not okay, la la la."

Mom came out of her bedroom. She said, "That song about not waking your parents just woke me up."

"Oops. Sorry," Mia said.

"Zeke, I'm glad you're reading books," Mom said. She smiled at me.

I glanced at the books in my hands. Mom seemed so happy. I didn't tell her I was just using the books to shield me from Alexa and her lavender nail polish. Instead, I said, "I'm bored."

"I told you not to use that word," Mom said.

"You told us we couldn't use it yesterday," I said. "Today I'm bored, bored, bored."

"I'm even more bored than you. You're bored, bored, bored. But I'm bored, bored, bored, bored," Alexa said.

"I have a great idea," I said. "You should play the Princess Sing-Along board game with Mia. It's fun," I lied.

Mia jumped up and down and yelled, "Yay!"

"Okay, I'll play with you," Alexa said.

I smiled. That would keep Alexa and her awful lavender polish away from my nails. And it would keep Mia and her awful board game away from me.

Now I just had to figure out what to do today. I invited my best friend, Hector, over.

Hector came to my house right away. "TV-Turnoff Week is so boring," he said.

"It sure is," I said. "What have you been doing?"

"I went to the science museum with my family yesterday. It was pretty fun," he admitted.

"I went to the art museum. It was pretty fun, too," I admitted. "But being home is boring."

"Yeah. But I got out my old train set. I liked that," he admitted.

"I found some toys in my bedroom closet. I liked that, too," I admitted. "But I miss the TV."

"I miss the TV, too," Hector said.

"I guess we could play outside," I said with
a sigh.

"I guess," he also said with a sigh.

Hector and I played basketball, Frisbee, and
hide-and-seek. We were outside for hours. I had
to admit it was a lot of fun.

Hector had to admit that, too.

Finally, we got so tired that we went inside. I sat on the couch and sighed again. "I wish we could watch TV or play video games now."

Hector sat next to me and sighed again, too. "Me too," he said.

"We could put on a pretend TV show," I said.

"It could be about two kids who aren't allowed to watch TV," Hector said.

"So they're really bored," I added.

"And also really smart, handsome, strong, and brave." Hector pounded on his chest.

Then he winced and said, "Ow. That hurts."

"One of the really smart, handsome, strong, and brave kids should be named Zeke," I said.

"Let's call the other really smart, handsome, strong, and brave kid Hector," Hector said.

We named our show "Hector and Zeke Save the World." I had wanted to call it "Zeke and Hector Save the World," but Hector won the coin toss.

We wore blankets for superhero capes. We used a bath towel as a cape for Waggles. Waggles played the role of Supermutt.

Next, we got martial arts weapons props. The weapons were really my yo-yo and pogo stick.

Then we rehearsed our show.

Alexa said, "I'll film your show for you."

"What about our Princess Sing-Along board game?" Mia asked Alexa. "We've been playing for hours. We're still not close to finishing."

Alexa yawned. "I quit the game. You win."

"I don't know why everyone keeps quitting the Princess Sing-Along game. But yay! I won another game!" Mia shouted. Then she asked me, "Now that the game is over, can I be in your movie?"

"Sure," I said. "You can be the bad guy. You drive your enemies crazy with your screechy songs."

"And you put your enemies to sleep with your boring game," Hector added.

We rehearsed some more. Then we performed our show for Mom.

I introduced the show with, "Ladies and
gentlemen." I looked at Mom. "Actually, just one
lady and no gentlemen. Let me start over."

I started over. "Lady. We will now put on
our show. It's called "Hector and Zeke Save the
World." It will be performed by Hector Cruz,
Zeke Meeks, Mia Meeks, and Waggles."

Hector and I bowed. Mia curtseyed. Waggles
drooled on the rug.

"The show is being filmed by Alexa Meeks in front of a large audience," I said.

"Don't call me large," Mom said.

"Okay. Sorry," I said. "Now Mia Meeks will sing the show's theme song." I moved back.

Mia came up front. She sang a Princess Sing-Along song. "Green boogers are gross in your nose, la la la. Worse than the gunk between your toes, la la la."

Then we put on our show. It went perfectly, except for three small things. One, when I swung my pogo stick, it hit the living room wall. Two, Waggles chewed a hole in his bath towel cape. And three, Alexa dropped the video recorder. But the hole in the wall from my pogo stick wasn't that big. And we had other bath towels.

And Alexa didn't destroy the video recorder on purpose.

Mom wasn't very happy about all that. In fact, she was very upset.

It took her a long time to calm down. Finally, she said, "You kids seemed to have a lot of fun today. You didn't need the TV or video games."

I realized I was smiling.

I quickly frowned. I said, "It's boring without TV and video games. Right, Hector?"

Hector stopped smiling, too. Then he said, "Uh, right."

I reminded myself to complain about being bored — even if I wasn't really bored.

There are BUGS in it!

On Monday morning, I got dressed, did another crossword puzzle, and played with my yo-yo.

Then I cleaned out my backpack. It had been a long time since I cleaned out my backpack. In fact, I don't think I have ever cleaned a backpack in my entire life.

I found a dime, a moldy apple with a dead worm sticking out of it, and this note from two girls in my class:

DEAR ZEKE,
YOU ARE SOOOOOO CUTE!
WE REALLY, REALLY, REALLY
WANT TO KISS YOU.
REALLY.
LOVE AND KISSES,
Nicole Finkle + Buffy Maynard

WHY ARE
GIRLS SO
GROSS?

Yuck. I shredded the disgusting note into
a zillion tiny pieces. Then I took the shredded
note out of my room and headed for the kitchen
trash can.

Mia was in the kitchen, eating Choco-Lard
cereal. She said, "I miss hearing Princess Sing-
Along on TV in the morning."

I did not miss hearing Princess Sing-Along in the morning. I didn't miss hearing her in the afternoon or nighttime either.

After breakfast, Mom drove my sisters and me to school. On the way, Mia sang a Princess Sing-Along song. "Please wear your seat belt on a trek, la la la. So you won't be a bloody wreck, la la la."

Yep. I did not miss the *Princess Sing-Along* show at all.

Once I got to school, I walked over to my friends on the playground. "Wasn't this weekend horrible without TV and video games?" I asked them.

"It sure was. Except for when my brother and I made chocolate fudge," Danny Ford said.

"It was horrible. Except when my dad played catch with me outside," Owen Leach said.

"My family went on a bike ride yesterday. It was fun. But I still miss the TV," Rudy Morse said.

"So everyone had a bad weekend," I said.

"I cried most of the time," Chandler Fitzgerald said. Then he started crying.

"Did you cry more than usual?" I asked him.

He shrugged.

"Playing warriors from *Fight, Fight, Fight* might cheer you up," I said.

"No. That will just remind me of the *Fight, Fight, Fight* TV show. Then I'll cry even harder," he said.

Then he cried even harder.

"Chandler's right," Owen said. "No one should play *Fight, Fight, Fight*."

"And we shouldn't say things from the *Sassy Sara* show, like 'Get lost.' It will remind us of the great TV shows we're missing," Laurie Schneider said.

So we didn't have any more fights or tell people to get lost. Now that we weren't fighting or sassing, we were actually nice to each other. It was very strange. But it was also kind of . . . well . . . nice.

My classmates gave their reports about what they did instead of watching TV. Chandler was first. He carried a big bottle of liquid to the front of the classroom.

THIS BOTTLE CONTAINS THE TEARS I'VE CRIED THE LAST FEW DAYS.

THE TEARS WEIGH EIGHTEEN AND A HALF OUNCES.

Then he took a bow.

Everyone clapped.

Everyone also rolled their eyes.

Grace Chang gave her report next. She wore lacy white gloves that matched her lacy white dress. She said, "Without the TV, I've had more time to sharpen my fingernails. I already had the sharpest nails in the world. But I've just beaten my own world record. I will now reveal my nails to you."

She put her hands behind her back. She slowly took off her gloves. They fell to the floor. Emma G. and Emma J. ran over and picked up the gloves. Then they raced back and laid the gloves neatly on Grace's desk.

Grace said, "I made my fingernails longer and sharper than ever. I also decorated them with bright pictures of knives, swords, and other weapons." She laughed evilly. Then she thrust out her hands.

My heart pounded. I gasped. I put my hand over my mouth so I wouldn't scream. I put my other hand over my chest so my heart wouldn't explode all over the place.

I am not going to describe Grace's nails to you. Trust me, I am doing you a big favor. Otherwise, you would probably have horrible nightmares about those gruesome nails for the rest of your life.

It was a huge relief when Grace sat down.

Rudy Morse walked to the front of the room next. I liked Rudy. He was really cool. He could cross his eyes, burp, and fart at the same time. The only things I didn't like about Rudy were his pet beetles. Beetles are insects. I'm terrified of insects.

Rudy said, "Don't worry. I won't scare you guys like Grace did."

"Grace didn't scare me," I said in a very shaky voice. Then I crawled out from under my desk.

"She didn't scare me either," a bunch of my classmates said in very shaky voices. They crawled out from under their desks.

I think Mr. McNutty crawled out from under his desk, too.

Rudy said, "Instead of watching TV or playing video games, I taught my sweet little pet some tricks."

Oh, no. I hoped Rudy wasn't talking about his pet beetle.

"I'm talking about my pet beetle," Rudy said.

Oh, no. I hoped he didn't mean the giant red one.

"I mean my giant red one," Rudy said.

I hoped he hadn't brought it to school.

"I brought it to school," Rudy said.

I hoped he wasn't going to show us the beetle.

"I'm going to show you my beetle," he said.

He opened his hand. On his palm was a giant red beetle. He said, "This is Cuddles."

I clapped. I hoped he was done.

"Stop clapping. I'm not done," Rudy said. "I want to show you Cuddles's newest trick."

I hoped Cuddles's newest trick was playing dead.

"Cuddles's newest trick is flying around the room," Rudy said.

I hoped he wouldn't get near me.

Cuddles flew around the room. He got near me.

Then he landed on my nose.

I screamed, "Yah! Ah! Gah! Wah, wah, wah!"

"Huh?" Rudy asked.

I screamed, "Get that thing off me!"

Rudy got Cuddles off me.

Then I screamed, "TV-Turnoff Week is the worst week ever!"

I was in a terrible mood for the rest of the day. At home, I was so bored that I even did all my homework. And for the first time in my life, I studied for a test.

Everyone in my family was in a bad mood. My sister Alexa was so bored that she weaved Waggles's fur into tiny braids.

Waggles barked. In dog language, it probably meant, "I'm in a bad mood, too. I'm bored and my fur looks ridiculous in tiny braids."

Mom and my sister Mia played the awful Princess Sing-Along board game. Mom kept telling Mia to hurry up. Mia kept telling Mom to stop telling her to hurry up.

"I'm so bored," I said.

"Play the Princess Sing-Along game with Mia," Mom said.

"No way. I'll never be that bored," I said.

"I'll pay you," Mom whispered.

"Game on!" I said.

BORED AGAIN.

I played the game for two hours. I had to stop before I died of boredom. Mom gave me five dollars.

I'd suffered without the TV and video games for three days. I still had four more days to go. I didn't know whether I could survive that long.

VISITING OTHER Planets Beats FLYING Around a Room

The next day, my class went to the library. As usual, I grabbed the shortest, lightest book I could find. I didn't care what it was about. I wasn't going to read it.

Then I sat at a big table and waited for my friends.

Hector, Owen, Aaron, and Danny soon came to my table. We talked, told jokes, and made fake fart noises. I loved library day.

Ms. Sohn, the librarian, came by. So I opened my book and pretended to read it.

"How's your book?" Ms. Sohn asked me.

"It's awesome. I love to read," I lied.

"You sure seem enthused about the history of bridal gowns," she said.

"Huh?" I asked.

"Your book is called *The History of Bridal Gowns*," the librarian said.

My friends laughed.

I closed the book. "I got this by mistake," I said.

"What book were you trying to get? *The History of Flower Girl Dresses*?" Owen asked.

My friends laughed even harder.

The librarian said, "I'll help you pick out a book, Zeke. Follow me."

My friends were still laughing when I went into the librarian's office.

"Do you like fiction or nonfiction?" Ms. Sohn asked me.

I shrugged.

"Contemporary or historical books?"

I shrugged.

"Realistic or fantasy?" the librarian asked.

Guess what I did next. Here's a hint: My shoulders really hurt. That's right. I shrugged again.

"Do you like to watch TV?" she asked.

I didn't shrug this time. Instead, I smiled and said, "I love TV."

"Tell me what shows you like best and why," she said.

I wondered what that had to do with books. But I did what the librarian asked. I said, "I like watching *The Talking Underwear* show because it's funny. I like *Wolfboy* because it's cool. And I like *Super Force Field* because it's about outer space."

"That's very helpful. You can return to your friends now," the librarian said.

So I headed back to my friends' table.

When Owen saw me coming, he sang, "Here comes the bride. Here comes the bride."

My friends laughed some more.

I scowled.

My friends stopped laughing when the librarian returned.

She set some books in front of me and said, "I got you a Captain Underpants book because you like humor. I chose *Enter the Zombie* for you because you like cool things. And I got a book called *Dwarf Planets* because you said you like outer space."

"Thank you," I said politely. I wouldn't read those books or any other books. But it was nice of Ms. Sohn to try to help me.

Then Hector said, "I love Captain Underpants. Ms. Sohn, can you pick out books for me, too?"

"I'd be happy to," she said.

Soon everyone else at the table asked for help. They all went to Ms. Sohn's office.

I sat alone at the table with a pile of books. I had no idea what to do. I sure wasn't going to read the books.

My teacher came by. "Why aren't you reading?" he asked me.

"I am," I lied. Then I opened the *Dwarf Planets* book and pretended to read the first page.

Then I really *did* read the first page. It was interesting.

Then I read the next page. It was interesting, too.

I kept on reading. When my friends returned, I showed them pictures from the book. "See this comet? It's also called a dwarf planet. And look at this weird asteroid," I said.

"That's cool. Can I read your book?" Hector asked.

"Not until I'm done with it," I said.

Then everyone read the books the librarian had picked out for them. It was very quiet at my table.

I was sorry when our class had to leave the library.

After we got back to our classroom, Victoria Crow gave her report. "TV-Turnoff Week doesn't bother me. I never watch TV or play video games anyway. That's one reason I'm the smartest kid in third grade," she said.

She held up a big metal thing with wide straps on it. She said, "This is a jetpack I made yesterday."

Then she strapped the jetpack on her back, pressed a button, and flew all over the classroom.

I liked watching Victoria fly around the room. It was much better than watching Rudy's giant red beetle fly around the room. Plus, Victoria didn't land on my nose.

After that, we took the test I had studied for at home. It was so easy that I finished it early.

Then I read a few more pages of the *Dwarf Planets* book. I couldn't wait to get home so I could finish it.

The next day at school, Mr. McNutty handed back our tests. I got my first perfect test ever. And what do you know? It was also the first test I'd ever studied for.

I showed my test to my family as soon as I got home.

Mom hugged me. "We should go out to celebrate your great test score," she said.

"Can we go to Hamburger Harry? It's a new restaurant. I heard it's good," my sister Alexa said.

"I want to go to Tunnels, Slides, and Balls Galore," I said.

"Yay!" my sister Mia yelled.

Alexa shook her head. "That place is for kids. I'm too old for Tunnels, Slides, and Balls Galore."

"Tunnels, Slides, and Balls Galore has greasy food. Also, it's loud and crowded," Mom said.

"I know. Greasy food and loud crowds are awesome," I said.

"Yay!" Mia yelled.

CRAZY PEOPLE

PEOPLE WHO LOVE GREASY FOOD AND LOUD CROWDS.

YES, WAGGLES COUNTS

"Let's try the new hamburger restaurant that Alexa heard about," Mom said.

Mom drove us to Hamburger Harry. On the way there, she asked Alexa, "What's so good about this restaurant?"

"I heard it's good," she replied.

"Is the food good?" Mom asked.

"I don't know," Alexa replied.

"Are the prices good?" Mom asked.

"I don't know," Alexa replied.

"Is the service good?" Mom asked.

"I don't know. I just heard the restaurant is good," Alexa replied.

We got to Hamburger Harry and went inside. Every wall in the restaurant was covered with TV screens.

"Yay!" Mia yelled.

"You just wanted to watch TV here, Alexa. You tried to trick me," Mom said. "Everyone get back in the car."

"So we're not going out to eat?" Alexa asked.

"We are," Mom said. Then she drove us to Tunnels, Slides, and Balls Galore.

"Yay!" Mia yelled.

"Yay!" I yelled.

"Boo!" Alexa yelled.

Mom put on earplugs and took some aspirin. Well, I think she wanted to at least.

Alexa crossed her arms and frowned.

Mia and I ate greasy pizza, salty french fries, and sugary shakes. We slid down slides, crawled through tunnels, threw balls, and shouted as loud as we could. We had a great time — even without TV or video games.

At school the next day, Mr. McNutty asked, "Did you all remember the big spelling bee today?"

Victoria Crow said, "I remembered."

Of course she did. She was the smartest kid in third grade.

Everyone else nodded and said they remembered the big spelling bee.

I nodded and said I remembered, too. But I was really thinking, "Ack! Yikes! Argh!" Also, "Whoa! Eek! Doy!" And "Yowza!" I'd forgotten all about the big spelling bee.

Victoria said, "I've been studying hard for the spelling bee. I'm going to win it."

Of course she would win it. She was the smartest kid in third grade.

I was not the smartest kid in third grade. I wasn't even in the top ten.

I hadn't been studying hard for the spelling bee. I hadn't been studying for it at all. I would probably be the first person to lose.

Everyone lined up against the classroom walls. Then Mr. McNutty gave each of us a word to spell.

The first round was easy. We had to spell words like *car*, *dog*, and *mat*. My word was *go*. It would be hard to misspell *go*. Everyone spelled their words correctly.

The second round got harder. Mr. McNutty told Aaron Glass to spell the word *glass*. He spelled it "g-l-a-s." He was the first one out.

Chandler Fitzgerald didn't know how to spell *happy*. That made him cry.

Then Grace Chang got the word *dust*. She spelled it "d-o-s-t."

"Sorry," the teacher said. "It's spelled 'd-u-s-t.'"

Grace said with a scowl, "It's not my fault. I've never dusted anything. Dusting could damage my long fingernails. Our maid always dusts for us. Can she come in and do the spelling bee for me?"

IF WE'RE LUCKY, SHE'LL BREAK A NAIL.

"No," Mr. McNutty said. Then he made Grace dust his desk.

Grace made Emma G. and Emma J. help her.

The spelling words got harder and harder. Many more kids had to sit down.

I got very nervous. I shuffled my feet from side to side.

Mr. McNutty said, "Zeke, your word is *spleen*."

I'd seen *spleen* in a word search I'd done this week. I spelled it right. Well, I didn't spell it "r-i-g-h-t." I spelled it "s-p-l-e-e-n." That was the right way to spell it.

Well, that's not the right way to spell *it*. *It* is spelled "i-t."

You know what I mean.

The next round got really hard. A lot of kids misspelled words and had to sit down.

I got even more nervous. I shuffled my feet harder and faster.

"Zeke, spell *python*," Mr. McNutty said.

I smiled. That was easy for me. I had read about pythons in my snake book.

I spelled *python* right.

Soon there were only a few people left in the spelling bee. Shockingly, I was one of them. I was so nervous I shuffled my feet even harder and faster.

"Zeke, do you need to go to the bathroom?" Mr. McNutty asked.

"No," I said. I felt myself blushing. I stopped shuffling my feet.

"All right. Spell the word *captain*," the teacher said.

"You mean like in Captain Underpants, the book I've been reading?" I asked.

"Yes," he said.

"C-a-p-t-a-i-n," I said.

"That's correct," the teacher said.

By then, the only kids still standing were Victoria Crow and me.

Mr. McNutty said, "Victoria, it's your turn. Spell *television*."

She frowned.

Watching TV came in handy sometimes. I knew how to spell *television*.

BUT I **NEVER** WATCH TELEVISION. THAT'S WHY I'M **SO SMART**. I DON'T CARE ABOUT TELEVISION, I **NEVER** PAY ATTENTION TO IT.

"Give it a try, Victoria," our teacher said.

She did. She spelled, "t-e-l-e-v-i-t-i-o-n."

"I'm sorry. That's wrong," Mr. McNutty said. "You'll have to sit down."

"But I'm the smartest kid in third grade," Victoria said.

"You aren't right now," Mr. McNutty said.

Victoria sat down.

Then the teacher turned to me. He said, "Zeke Meeks, if you spell the next word correctly, you'll win the class spelling bee. It's a hard one. Ready?"

I nodded, though I didn't think I'd ever be ready.

He said, "Spell *asteroid.*"

That wasn't a hard one. I'd just seen that word in the *Dwarf Planets* book. I closed my eyes and pictured the word in the book. Then I said, "a-s-t-e-r-o-i-d."

"Congratulations, Zeke. You won the spelling bee," Mr. McNutty said.

Everyone clapped for me.

Hector yelled out, "Wahoo for Zeke!"

Chandler Fitzgerald cried even harder. "I wanted to win!" he sobbed.

Victoria asked, "How did you win, Zeke? You're not the smartest kid in third grade. You're not even in the top ten."

I said, "I've been reading books and doing word searches and crossword puzzles. I guess that helped."

Mr. McNutty gave me my prize: a gift certificate to Cheeseham's Best Bookstore. Cheeseham's Best Bookstore was also Cheeseham's *only* bookstore.

"This is great!" I said. I wanted to get a book about lizards, another Captain Underpants book, and a new crossword puzzle book.

Then I remembered that TV-Turnoff Week would be over in two days. I could watch TV and play video games again. I wouldn't need to read books.

But I thought I might want to anyway.

World's Longest REPORT and Shortest MATH LESSON

I gave my report the next day. I carried a large box to the front of the classroom and said, "I missed watching TV and playing video games this week."

"Me too!" Chandler sobbed.

"Luckily, I found some stuff in my closet to keep me busy," I said. I took my crossword puzzle book and word search book out of the box. I showed the class some of the puzzles I'd done.

Then I said, "I played with my yo-yo too. Let me show you some tricks." I took the yo-yo out of the box. I showed the class a throw down and a breakaway.

Mr. McNutty said, "Good job, Zeke. Now finish up, so I can start the math lesson."

Math lesson? Yuck. I didn't want to finish my report for that. "I'll just do one more trick," I said. I performed a very slow walk the dog.

Mr. McNutty started clapping.

I said, "I forgot about the reverse sleeper."
I did that trick.

"All right, Zeke. Sit down," Mr. McNutty said.
"Now everyone get out your math books."

"I'm not done with my report. I did so much
stuff this week," I said. I took a five-dollar bill
out of my box. "I earned five dollars for playing
the most boring game in the world with my little
sister."

"Zeke, we need to start the math lesson,"
Mr. McNutty said.

I took out a postcard from the art museum
and said, "I haven't talked about the art
museum yet. I saw some cool paintings there."

Next I took my books out of the box. "I finished *Dwarf Planet*, Captain Underpants, and a book about snakes. I just started reading *Enter the Zombie* this morning," I said.

"That is enough, Zeke. Sit down," the teacher said.

"Okay. Let me put everything back in the box." I did — very, very slowly.

"Hurry up so we can get to our math lesson," Mr. McNutty said.

"Okay," I said. Then I tipped over the box, making everything spill out. "Oops," I said, trying not to laugh.

"Ezekiel Meeks. Do I have to send you to the principal's office?" the teacher asked.

"No," I said. I quickly put everything back and returned to my seat.

Mr. McNutty said, "Finally! Now get out your math books."

OOPS!!!

"Isn't anyone going to clap for me?" I asked.

The class started clapping. They kept clapping and clapping and clapping. They must not have wanted to do math either.

They didn't stop clapping until the bell rang for school to let out.

Mr. McNutty sighed. "You can go home now," he said.

I smiled.

"Except for you, Zeke," he said. "You'll be staying after school today to do extra math problems."

I guess I deserved that.

I stopped smiling and got out my math book.

A Sound WORSE Than the One in My STOMACH

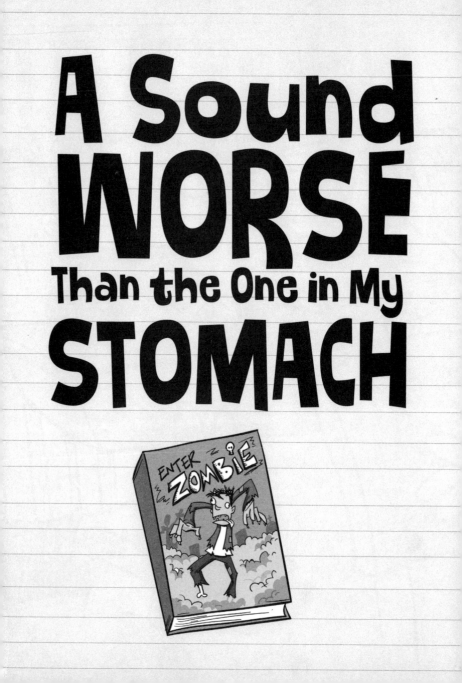

I woke up early Saturday morning. I stayed
in bed and read a few more chapters of *Enter the
Zombie*. It was a really funny book.

Then I did another crossword puzzle. I
couldn't figure out one of the clues: a seven-
letter word meaning "happy." The first letter
was C.

Do you know what the word is? If so, you're
probably smarter than me. But I'm still probably
better at spelling than you.

I looked up the word *happy* in my dictionary. Aha! I found the answer.

Do you know what seven-letter word starts with a C and means "happy?" You can probably find it in your dictionary. Go ahead.

Think.

Ready?

The seven-letter word that starts with a C and means "happy" is . . .

. . . ARE YOU SURE YOU'RE READY?

Okay, the seven-letter word that starts with a C and means "happy" is *pluck*.

Did you already figure out it was *pluck*?

If you did, that would be really weird. *Pluck* starts with a P and has five letters and doesn't even mean "happy." I was kidding about the word being *pluck*.

Actually, the answer is *content*. I hope that makes you content.

Now where was I? Oh, yeah. I was telling you about looking through the dictionary on Saturday morning.

THANK YOU, MR. DICTIONARY!

So after I found *content* in the dictionary, I gave the dictionary a little thank-you hug.

You probably think it's dorky to give a dictionary a thank-you hug. You're probably right.

I also started reading the dictionary.

You probably think that reading the dictionary is dorky, too. But it was fun. I saw the word *feces* in there. That's another word for poop. And I learned what a pustule is. It's a pimple full of puss. I also saw the word *gruesome* in the dictionary. Next to it was a picture of Grace Chang's fingernails. Seeing that was not fun.

Now where was I again?

Oh, yeah. So I read part of the dictionary.

Then I wrote *content* in my crossword puzzle.

Then I heard a weird growling sound.

Yikes! Was there a monster in my room? Or a wild animal that had escaped from the zoo? Or an alien from outer space?

Then I realized what was making the weird growling sound: my stomach. I was hungry.

I looked at my clock. It was already ten o'clock. I had been awake for hours and hadn't even eaten yet.

I left my room and walked toward the kitchen.

My sister Alexa was watching a TV show in the living room. She was also hugging and kissing the TV.

"You're going to get in trouble for watching TV," I said. She shook her head.

TV–TURNOFF WEEK IS **OVER!**

Oh, yeah. I'd forgotten all about that. "Can I watch a TV show now?" I asked.

"After this concert is over. Isn't Foxy Duchess Stargirl an amazing singer?" Alexa asked. She pointed to the TV.

"She's amazingly bad," I said.

Foxy Duchess Stargirl was making growling sounds even weirder than the sounds from my stomach.

I did not like having the TV on right then.

"Princess Sing-Along is a much better singer than Foxy Duchess Stargirl," Mia said. Then she screeched, "Wash your hands well before you eat, la la la. Unless you like dirt in your meat, la la la."

I left the room. I walked into the kitchen and ate a big bowl of cereal. Then I went outside and played with my neighbors.

When I got back home, Mia was watching *Princess Sing-Along* on TV.

Mia and the princess screeched, "Do not scratch your sores, my dear, la la la, or nasty scabs will appear, la la la."

I did not like having the TV on then either.

I went to my bedroom. I practiced yo-yo tricks and did a word search puzzle. Then I made a cool sword out of LEGOs. Hector and I could use the sword for the next show we performed.

Finally, I returned to the living room and watched two episodes of *Wolfboy* on TV. I mean, it's not like I was never going to watch TV again.

The school librarian had been right. The *Wolfboy* TV show was a lot like the *Enter the Zombie* book she'd gotten for me. I clicked off the TV and read more of my *Enter the Zombie* book.

TV and video games were fun. But so were books, toys, games, and lots of other things!

ABOUT THE AUTHOR

D. L. Green lives in California with her husband, three children, silly dog, and a big collection of rubber chickens. She loves to read, write, and joke around.

ABOUT THE ILLUSTRATOR

Josh Alves didn't watch a lot of TV growing up. Instead, he spent his time reading, drawing, learning sleight-of-hand magic tricks, and how to juggle. Constantly doodling, Josh eventually grew up, married an awesome woman, and gets to draw with his three kids in his studio in Maine.

COULD YOU SURVIVE A WEEK WITHOUT TV?
(And other really important questions)

Write answers to these questions, or discuss them with your friends and classmates.

1. Could you survive a week without TV? What would you do? How much extra time would you have on your hands? Would you like it or HATE it?

2. Of all the things I did during TV-Turnoff Week, which was the most impressive? New yo-yo tricks? Hector's and my show? Winning the spelling bee or something else?

3. What sort of rules do your parents have for TV watching? Do you think they are good rules? If you could set the rules, what would they be?

4. It was totally awesome when I won the spelling bee. Have you ever done anything like that?

BIG WORDS
according to Zeke

TRY USING THEM IN SENTENCES JUST LIKE I DO

ADMITTED: Finally told what you REALLY did or how you REALLY feel about something. Admitting something can be really hard to do.

ANNOUNCEMENTS: Big, important news that can either be super great (a new *Fight, Fight, Fight* video game coming soon) or super terrible (math test on Friday).

ASTEROID: A small planet — some would call it dwarflike — with a diameter ranging from less than a kilometer to almost 800 kilometers. There are thousands of them between Mars and Jupiter. I wish Grace Chang would move to one of them.

AUDIENCE: The crowd of people who watch you do something amazing. Your audience could also be just your mom.

CONTEMPORARY: Hip, new, fresh, and happening today! A contemporary book about cool kids would HAVE to show them playing video games, watching *Fight, Fight, Fight*, and having fun at recess. (Hint: The Zeke Meeks books are very contemporary.)

CURTSEYED: Bowed or kneeled in a weird, stuffy way. Girls do it when they are acting like princesses.

THIS IS THE PERFECT
EXAMPLE OF SOMETHING.
DISGUSTING AND
EXTREMELY GRUESOME.

DISGUSTING: Things that make you go "EW!" like love
notes, most girls, and liver.

EXTREMELY: Super-duper, very much so.

GRUESOME: Something that causes horror or extreme
fear! Think Grace Chang's fingernails.

INVISIBLE: Something that you can't see. I wish I could
be invisible every time Grace Chang's gruesome fingernails
were near me.

MUSEUM: A place that seems boring at first, but when
you start looking, you see that it is filled with collections
and displays that are super cool. You tend to learn a lot at
museums, but they are still fun.

RIDICULOUS: Very silly and just not right, like Waggles in
girly clothes.

TEDIOUS: If something is tedious, it makes you tired
because it is extremely boring or it takes a long time or
probably both. Think TV-Turnoff Week. (See also tiresome.)

TIRESOME: If something is tiresome, it makes you tired
because it is extremely boring or it takes a long time or
probably both. Think TV-Turnoff Week. (See also tedious.)

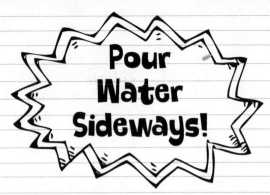

Pour Water Sideways!

When you can't watch TV, you end up with tons of extra time. It is important to keep busy, though, or else your mom might make you play Princess Sing-Along games. Magic tricks are fun to do. Plus, you can eat up time by practicing AND performing them. This one will especially impress your mom and dad because it doubles as a science experiment.

What you need:

- a three-feet long piece of yarn

- a liquid measuring cup with spout

- a drinking glass

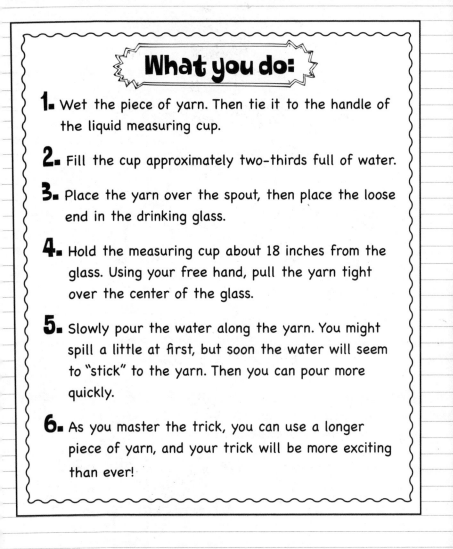

What you do:

1. Wet the piece of yarn. Then tie it to the handle of the liquid measuring cup.

2. Fill the cup approximately two-thirds full of water.

3. Place the yarn over the spout, then place the loose end in the drinking glass.

4. Hold the measuring cup about 18 inches from the glass. Using your free hand, pull the yarn tight over the center of the glass.

5. Slowly pour the water along the yarn. You might spill a little at first, but soon the water will seem to "stick" to the yarn. Then you can pour more quickly.

6. As you master the trick, you can use a longer piece of yarn, and your trick will be more exciting than ever!

Why it works: Water molecules like to stick together. When you wet the yarn in step one, you make a liquid surface for the water to cling to.

AWESOME HAIR

CHARMING SMILE

COOLEST THIRD GRADER YOU'LL EVER MEET!

WWW.CAPSTONEKIDS.COM